D0245140

This Orchard
book belongs to

....

....

For Dee

www.alisonmurray.net

ORCHARD BOOKS
338 Euston Road, London NW1 3BH
Orchard Books Australia
Level 17/207 Kent Street, Sydney, NSW 2000

First published in 2014 by Orchard Books
First paperback publication in 2015

ISBN 978 1 40831 307 7

A CIP catalogue record for this book is available from the British Library.

1 3 5 7 9 10 8 6 4 2

Printed in China

Orchard Books is a division of Hachette Children's Books,
an Hachette UK company.
www.hachette.co.uk

The House That ZAC BUILT

Alison Murray

ORCHARD

This is the house that Zac built.

And this is the fly that **BUZZED** on by over the house that Zac built.

This is the cat
that stalked the fly
that **BUZZED** on by
over the house that Zac built.

This is the cream way up high,

approached by the cat . . .

. . . who followed the fly

that BUZZED on by
over the house that Zac built.

This is the dog, deep in a dream . . .

. . . till

DOWN

came
the jug

and SPLASH went the cream . . . .

. . . spilt by the cat
with her head held high,
who was still determined
to catch that fly . . .

. . . which

BUZZED on by

over the house

that Zac built.

These are the lambs, calm and serene . . .

Then along came the dog,
all covered in cream . . .

who raced through the farm
when roused from his dream,

. . . ignored by the cat,
who despite all that

kept her eye on the fly
as it BUZZED on by . . .

and
STOPPED . . .

on the house
that Zac built.

Zac looked around
and gasped in alarm
when he saw the MESS
they had made on the farm!

But Zac was smart,
he knew what to do.

He patted the dog who
was trusty and true.

He collected more cream
from Daisy and then . . .

. . . he herded the lambs back into their pen.

With the cat in his arms
and the farm like new . . .

. . . he took a deep breath

and BLEW!

Off buzzed the fly,
'Meow' went the cat,
'Woof' went the dog,
and down they all sat

and gazed amazed
at the house
that Zac built.